Ramón and His Mouse

Margarita Robleda
Illustrated by Maribel Suárez

Originally published in Spanish as *Ramón y su ratón*
Adaptation of stories and songs to English: Georgette Baker

2105 NW 86th Avenue
Miami, FL 33122
www.santillanausa.com

Managing Editor: Isabel Mendoza

Alfaguara is part of the **Santillana Group**,
with offices in the following countries:
ARGENTINA, BOLIVIA, CHILE, COLOMBIA, COSTA RICA, DOMINICAN REPUBLIC, ECUADOR, EL SALVADOR, GUATEMALA, MEXICO, PANAMA, PARAGUAY, PERU, PUERTO RICO, SPAIN, UNITED STATES, URUGUAY, AND VENEZUELA.

Ramon and His Mouse
ISBN 10: 1-59820-993-0
ISBN 13: 978-1-59820-993-8

Published in the United States of America
Printed in Colombia by D'vinni S.A.

10 09 08 07   1 2 3 4 5 6 7 8 9 10

For César Alejandro Mendivil Robleda

Ramón had a vase in his house.

Under the floor lived a skinny mouse.

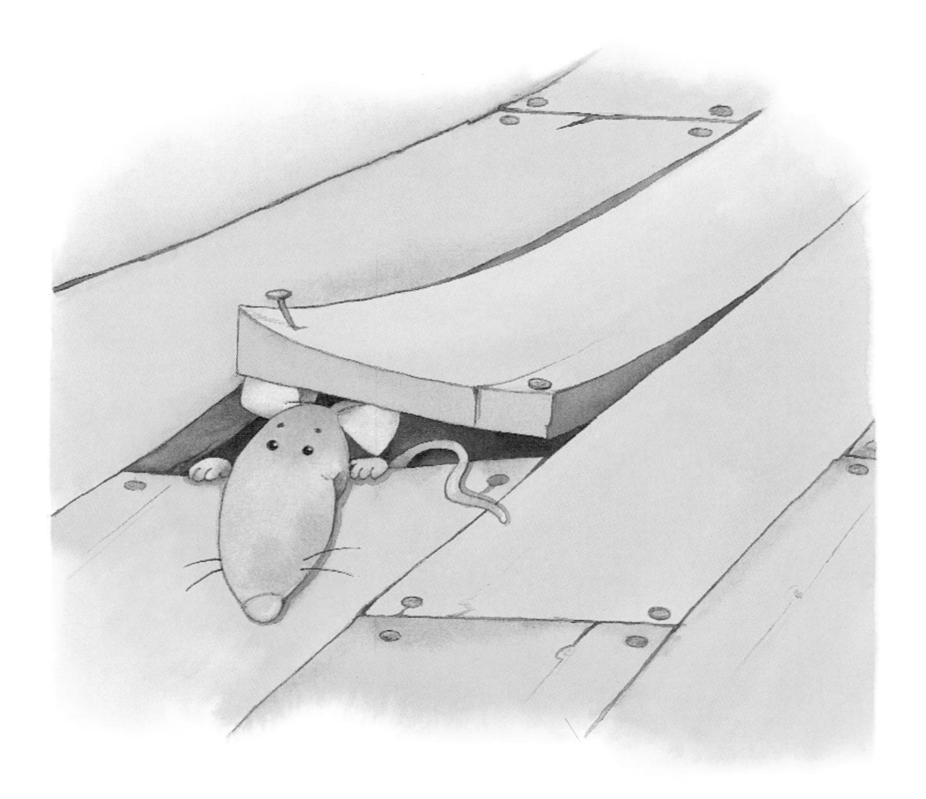

On a special day, Ramón got a ham.

So the little mouse wouldn't eat up the ham,

Ramón thought, “I’ll hide it, while I can.”

The clever mouse found it after breaking the vase.

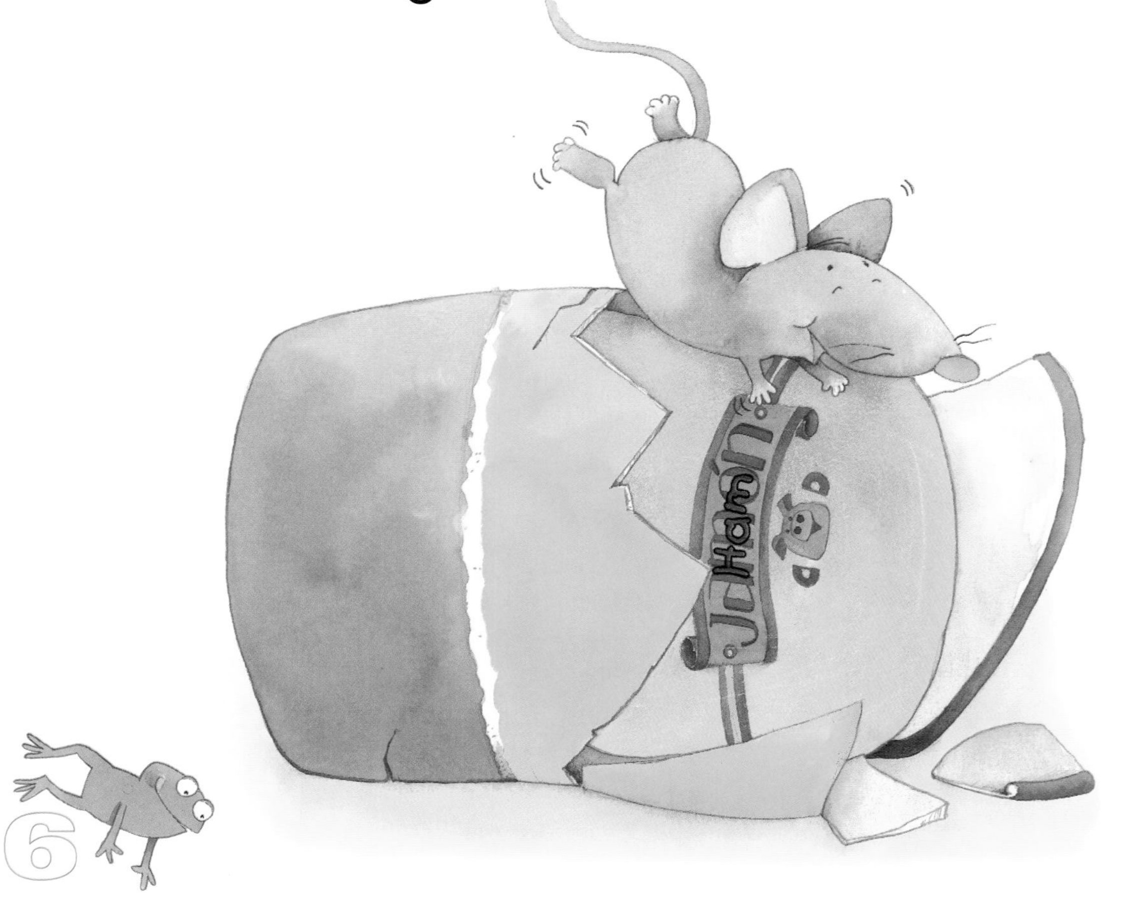

As quickly as he could,
the mouse stuffed his face!

Now, Ramón has lost his only vase,

and lives with a mouse in his old house...

while the ham is in the tummy
of the fat, happy mouse!

The Authors

Margarita Robleda likes to be called "Rana Margarita de la Paz y la Alegría" (Frog Margarita of Peace and Happiness). She is a Mexican writer who loves to play with words and use them to tickle her readers, both young and old. She has more than 75 published books. She also has books of riddles and tongue twisters in Spanish. In this collection, this frog rows and plays with rhymes, and her only wish is to make you smile.

Maribel Suárez was born in Mexico City. She studied Industrial Design and received her Masters in Design Studies at the Royal College of Art, in London, England. She has been illustrating children's books for about 20 years, and she enjoys it very much.

And they all lived happily ever after...
This dream became a reality
with the effort and teamwork of many people,
and it was printed by:

D'vinni S.A.
Bogotá - Colombia 2007